Adrian Clark was born in East Sussex and was raised by a foster family. Educated in Bexhill-on-Sea. Left school at sixteen, with no formal qualifications. An ordinary man from an ordinary background, which goes to show that there is a book inside all of us.

Later, Adrian moved to Devon, where he developed a love of people and human nature, along with travel and a sense of humour.

Dedicated to my wife and travel partner, Sylvie, who is my inspiration.

Adrian Clark

PURA VIDA

AUSTIN MACAULEY PUBLISHERS™
LONDON • CAMBRIDGE • NEW YORK • SHARJAH

Copyright © Adrian Clark (2020)

The right of Adrian Clark to be identified as author of this work has been asserted by him in accordance with section 77 and 78 of the Copyright, Designs and Patents Act 1988.

All rights reserved. No part of this publication may be reproduced, stored in a retrieval system or transmitted in any form or by any means, electronic, mechanical, photocopying, recording or otherwise, without the prior permission of the publishers.

Any person who commits any unauthorised act in relation to this publication may be liable to criminal prosecution and civil claims for damages.

A CIP catalogue record for this title is available from the British Library.

ISBN 9781788488815 (Paperback)
ISBN 9781788488822 (Hardback)
ISBN 9781528954969 (ePub e-book)

www.austinmacauley.com

First Published (2020)
Austin Macauley Publishers Ltd
25 Canada Square
Canary Wharf
London
E14 5LQ

Preface

It has been said that everyone will get their 15 minutes of fame. It has also been said that inside everyone there is a book.

Here, I am putting it to the test, although that is not my reason for writing this book.

Before going to Costa Rica, there was very little written about the country, apart from the usual rough guides, which I find quite difficult to navigate.

I dedicate this book to my wife Sylvie for her support and her sense of adventure that made this book possible.

An Introduction to Costa Rica

Costa Rica is one of those countries that are on the peripheral of our consciousness. It's not one of those you hear about on the BBC.

Costa Rica is part of the narrow strip of land that makes up Central America. It lies between Nicaragua and Panama.

It has a population of 4.5 million people, a quarter of whom live in and around the capital, San José.

At the mention of Central America, you might think that Costa Rica is a third world country, full of poverty and revolutions. If so, you are very wrong. With its export of bananas, coffee and cocoa, and its boom in eco-tourism, it is a very wealthy country.

What does it do with this income?

Since 1949, Costa Rica has no military force, no army. It is in a pact with other American countries. If you strike Costa Rica, the other Americans hit back they are very well defended.

This means that they can spend their income on the infrastructure, especially their education system, every child has access to schools and universities.

The country is made up of tropical rainforests, volcanoes (Arenal is the most well-known and active), raging rivers and lakes (Arenal being the largest).

It has a year-round tropical climate, which means a lot of rain. Around 25% of the land area is in protected national parks (which is the highest percentage in the world).

The wildlife of Costa Rica includes big cats (look out for jaguars), tapirs, four species of monkey, including white-headed capuchin, the mantled howler, spider monkey and the squirrel monkey. Add to these the varieties of sloth, turtles and river otters.

There are over 840 species of birds in Costa Rica including the national bird, the quetzal. Other species include the macaw and the toucan.

Then, to conclude the list, there are hundreds of varieties of lizards, snakes, spiders and insects.

For excitement, adventure and wildlife on every corner, Costa Rica is the place to visit.

Chapter One
From Little Acorns

Who would have thought that watching a game of football could be so life changing? The game in question was in the world cup of 2014 in Brazil. It was a group match between England and Costa Rica, which ended as a 0-0 draw.

There I was in the zone, passing the ball, putting in the tackles, and scoring the goals, from the comfort of my sofa.

Sylvie, my long-suffering wife, although sitting beside was in an entirely different zone altogether, suddenly jumped up, and made her way to the bookcase.

Armed with research books and tuned into the internet, she started her homework.

"Did you know that Costa Rica is about the same size as Wales?" says Sylvie, "Costa Rica is translated as Rich Coast, and is one of the most developed countries in Central America. It is covered in the tropical rain forest, and is full of wildlife."

We have been married for 18 years, so I knew what that meant. Further investigation was needed so off we went to the travel agents. We picked on Virgin Holidays as this was quite a unique holiday, not our usual two weeks on the beach.

We told them what we wanted, they told us what they had, which seemed reasonable, at a price we liked. So for now, all we could do was save.

A few months pass, when suddenly, out of the blue, on my home from work, our plan changes. There in the window of a major high street travel agent, were pictures and an advert for Costa Rican tours.

Going to Costa Rica was to be a special holiday, so it had to be done properly. As a result, the 11-day adventure tour seemed perfect. So now we had a plan. Therefore, we kept on saving.

Costa Rica is rugged rain forested country in Central America with coastlines on the Caribbean Sea to the east, and the Pacific Ocean to the west.

It has two seasons, the wet season, from May to November, and the dry season (it still rains, but not as much) from December to April.

We decided in February 2016. Okay, so now what to pack. Our Adventure Tour would include volcanoes, rivers, beaches and rain forests.

When on holiday in the med we usually unpack at the hotel. On this holiday, we would be moving on every couple of days, lugging suitcases behind us.

Sylvie brought herself a new suitcase with a pretty butterfly pattern, very Costa Rican, which she fills with sensible, practical clothes.

I, on the other hand, have an ordinary suitcase, which I fill with a new bush hat, a new bush jacket with so many pockets I kept losing things, and the loudest shirts anyone could find. I had turned into a Del Boy.

At this stage, Sylvie brings health issues to the table. More research needed. After a visit to the doctors, Sylvie decides to take anti-malarial tablets. Me? Oh, I'll be all right.

Hold on, we've forgotten about the money. We need some cash. What is their currency?

In Costa Rica, they use the colon, as well as the American dollar. So a quick trip to the post office to arrange our pocket money.

So packed and medicated, the adventure begins. Oh! By the way, we are not as young as we think we are.

Chapter Two
The Journey

The day was fast approaching, the excitement was building. What have we let ourselves in for?

It started quietly enough with a train journey from Newton Abbot to Heathrow Airport, and a night at an airport hotel. A very pleasant experience, which meant that we felt refreshed and ready for our long flight.

We started with a nine-hour flight to Houston, Texas. (No dream liner for us.) We were flying with United Airlines with all the mod-cons.

We passed the time keeping a check on the flight map.

When we flew over Canada, it looked bleak and barren. We also watched some in-flight movies (I lost count of the number of James Bond films available), interspersed with eating, drinking and the occasional walk-about.

Sylvie is a very strict vegetarian, and so ordered a veggie meal. Unfortunately, she ordered one for me (a meat eater) as well, although I don't think it would have made much of a difference, nobody knew what they were eating. Animal, vegetable or mineral?

Eventually, we landed at Houston. Part one was completed. Time for an intermission. The only problem was, one man's intermission is another man's culture shock.

Whilst on the plane we filled out a customs questionnaire, as to what foods and cereals, or other plant life we might be bringing into the country.

As we disembark and go through the customs hall, we are separated from the other passengers because we were travelling on.

We now approached a machine that asked a lot of questions, photographed our faces, and took our fingerprints.

A short walk saw us face to face with an American customs officer. Same questions, same fingerprints, and same photograph, only with a sense of humour. I think I preferred the machine. None the less, we could now enter the United States.

It's time now to experience some American cuisine. For large people, they have small portions. I went for something meaty, washed down with root beer. Sylvie, of course, had a salad.

If getting into the country was difficult, leaving was even more so especially for Devon country bumpkins. Shoes off, belts off, electronic devices out, hands up, assume the position. Flash, bang, wallop. After two hours in the United States, we could now leave.

Part two of our great adventure was a three and a quarter hour flight to San José, Costa Rica. A very quiet affair. No food unless you pay, no drinks unless you pay and no entertainment unless you pay. Time for a nap.

We touched down in San José at one in the morning, local time (Costa Rica is six hours behind the UK).

We went through passport control, found our luggage, and met our guide, who had been waiting for us. Easy.

We got to our hotel at about two in the morning. A total journey time, from house to hotel of 33 hours.

Nevertheless, we are now in Costa Rica.

Chapter Three
San José

In 1821, Costa Rica gained independence from Spain, which was followed by a power struggle between four main cities. In 1835, after two wars, San José was declared the capital San José sits 12,000 metres above sea level on a plateau in the Central Valley. It is surrounded by the lush green Talamanca Mountains to the south and the volcanoes to the north.

April is the hottest month of the year with an average temperature of 25 degrees, whereas, January is decidedly chilly at 22 degrees. The wettest month is September with an average rainfall of some 240 millimetres. The driest month, there's is no such thing.

The city is distinguished by its Spanish colonial buildings, like the ornate, neo-classical National Theatre of Costa Rica, overlooking the downtown Plaza de la Cultura, a popular gathering spot.

Below the Plaza is the Pre-Columbian Gold Museum, with its display of hundreds of gleaming artefacts.

We wake up at six o'clock, after four hours of sleep. I don't know whether it was the noise of the birds or the early morning crowds that came past our hotel that woke us. The square outside is so alive.

We are staying at the four-star Grand Hotel in downtown San José. It was constructed between 1928 and 1930, in the neoclassical style with brick and cement. It was originally four floors with a small tower. Later, a fifth floor

was added. For many years, it was the most distinguished Hotel in San José, with many famous people staying there. "Did you know?" chirps Sylvie, "Did you know that President Kennedy stayed here? (In the Presidential Suite)"

It was built full of splendour and magnificence, but now it was beginning to show its age.

From the outside, it was putting on a brave face, with its blue-grey façade, its large windows and its outside café culture seating area surrounded by coffee shrubs.

Once inside, the stars just fell away, which was oh! So sad, as there were signs of a glorious history.

Anyway, it's time for breakfast. As we make our way to the dining room, the first thing that grabs you is its size. With its large windows, luxurious drapes and the opulent chandelier lighting, it looks beautiful. You could imagine dancing the waltz here in times gone by.

Looking lost in the corner of the dining room, there was a small buffet table loaded down with cereals, fruit, eggs and rolls, the usual breakfast fare. Taking centre stage though, in the middle of the table, was the ubiquitous rice and black beans. Our stomachs weren't quite ready, a bit early in the day for us for this treat. We'll try them later.

We spied a harassed young lady cooking omelettes. She was kept very busy, but they were delicious.

Stomachs satisfied, it was time to explore the city. For being the capital, it was surprisingly quiet, certainly quieter than earlier in the morning.

It is a bright, sunny day. It is like an early summer's day in the Med. Not bad for February.

In the area around the hotel, there is a museum and a theatre, but this morning we decided to go to the Parque La Sabana.

This 72-hectare park was once San José main airport and is now the lungs of the city. The park has many facilities including Costa Rica's national football stadium.

Despite its size, we couldn't find it. Maybe we were so near yet so far away. So anyway, we decided to back to the hotel for coffee.

We had come to Costa Rica to see the wildlife, but the only wildlife we are seeing are pigeons, (as seen back home).

"Let's try some culture," suggests Sylvie, "Let's go to the Pre-Columbian Gold Museum."

The Pre-Columbian Gold Museum is housed in the Plaza de la Cultura and Banco Central Museum.

"Wow! What a mouth full," says Sylvie.

This museum was built in 1982 and is as much as 40 feet deep. It also houses the Central Bank Coin Collection Museum, a library, an auditorium and an open area for exhibitions and other events.

All this has made me hungry.

"Not until we have been to the Pre-Columbian Museum," Sylvie tells me.

It is housed under the main road and square. It is an interesting museum showing how the people lived before the Spanish turned up.

On reflection, after visiting the museum, we feel that the Spanish did not benefit the people. The quality of life that they enjoyed appeared to have been very good. From what we could see they were better off being left alone, but hey! That would not have been progress.

By now, our stomachs are letting us know it is lunch time. Where should we go? What should we eat? We have not seen a restaurant, a gastropub, or even a café.

"I know," says Sylvie, "let's go to the theatre."

Of course, Sylvie is right. In downtown San José, the theatre is one of the best and most popular places for lunch.

The ambience is very welcoming, and the fare was very tasty. Again, we declined the black beans and rice. How long can we hold out?

The National Theatre of Costa Rica was constructed between 1890 and 1897 and is one of the finest buildings in San José.
Built in brick and stone at the base, with granite and marble walls. The exterior displays allegories of dance, music, and fame. (The ones you see are replicas.)
The floor was specifically built on a cantilever style so that the whole floor can be raised on special international occasions.

After lunch, we decided to do a tour of the theatre. It is a beautiful building, which like our hotel, belongs to another era.

If you, the reader, think I am being a bit negative, you may be right, but I feel that these beautiful buildings need looking after.

When visiting dignitaries visit the country, they stay at the Grand Hotel and have functions at the National Theatre. Does this mean that my Sylvie is a VIP? I think so.

It is now four o'clock, time to move to another hotel.

We don't know why, it was not explained, but we are moving four blocks to the Holiday Inn.

Instead of trying to find a restaurant in town, we decided to have dinner in the hotel. There are two restaurants in the Holiday Inn. The one on the top floor was jammed packed with an American party, so we head downstairs to a much quieter restaurant, (us and one other couple).

"I think they're on our tour," Sylvie speculated, with no clues that I could see.

Meanwhile, we take a look at the menu, and hey presto!

Black beans and rice. All right then, we'll give them a go. Turns out they're not bad.

We have an early start in the morning, so an early night is in order. (No sign of any jet lag.) We have not yet unpacked, not sure when, or if we will.

Chapter Four
Tortuguero

It's six o'clock in the morning. The tour starts here. We start our day with a coffee and a croissant, then go and meet up with the rest of the party.

There are 12 of us plus a guide and driver. We enter the reception area to a cacophony of noise, there are people and baggage everywhere. It's like a community centre in a disaster zone. It becomes a guessing game as to who is with us. Sylvie was of course right the previous evening, the couple we saw were indeed members of our party. It was quite reassuring to know we weren't the oldest on our tour.

Six thirty and our minibus arrives. Our driver is Juan.

Quiet and dependable. Our guide is Adonys. Sounds Greek, looks like an older version of Joey from *Friends*.

We all introduce ourselves and begin to bond into 'the gang' as I call us. A breakfast stop is arranged for eight o'clock. Time to get to know the gang.

Then Adonys interjects with a question, "How many volcanoes are there in Costa Rica?"

"Three," I shout out. You see I have done my research.

"Give Adrian a big hand," says Adonys. There is cheering and clapping in loud applause.

"Wrong!" says Adonys, "There are over 100." Cheering and clapping now turns into wild laughter. Ice definitely broken.

"As a precaution, the buildings outside the cities have tin roofs in case of a volcano eruption. (Tin is safer than tiles and will cause less personal injury.)"

"In Costa Rica, we all say 'pura vida'. All repeat." We all obey. "It is used when we say thank you, and goodbye, but it is much more than that. It is the way of life. Pure life."

"What wildlife are you hoping to see on this tour?" we are asked.

I choose sloths, Sylvie goes for racoons, the rest of the gang go for others such as jaguars, poison frogs, toucans, parrots and crocodiles. I know, we are such a demanding group, but why not aim high.

Adonys makes a list, and as we enter the rainforest all eyes are peeled.

Okay, our guide and driver have matters in hand, and we are one happy gang as we go to breakfast

Of course, there are rice and black beans on the menu.

They feature very heavily on every menu. Breakfast, lunch and dinner.

During breakfast, Adonys casually mentions that Juan has found sloths outside in the grounds.

Out we pour with cameras and binoculars in hand. It doesn't take us long to spot a mother three-toed sloth, with a baby on her back, high in the tree.

High in another tree, we spotted a four-toed sloth, and in the undergrowth, we find blue jeans frogs, so called because although their heads and torso are bright red, their lower half and legs are bright blue as if they are wearing blue jeans. Animal counting has begun.

Not only are there wild animals on the grounds, but also wild plants. We are shown a very old tree. We are told that it is a 300-year-old kapok tree.

As we continue our journey, we pass many banana plantations. At one stage, we pulled off to the side of the road and took a walk in amongst the bananas.

"Why are some wrapped in blue plastic?" asked Sylvie.

These are ready for harvesting, the plastic is to keep the spiders out. (We'll talk bananas later.)

We then come to the end of the road, literally, at La Pavona. From here, we have to take a boat, which is not as straight forward as it may appear. Between the road and the river is mud.

If you get there early the mud is quite firm. So with a suitcase in hand, we race down to our boat, and then watch the chaos unfold.

If you pay one dollar, a barefooted local will carry your bags to the boat. This gets very competitive, with the mud getting softer and softer, and the guys slipping and sliding all over the place. Very amusing.

I suppose the obvious question is—why not improve the riverbank?

If they did, we would all carry our own bags, and the locals would be out of business.

The boats carry around forty passengers, plus luggage. It takes up to two hours to get to Tortuguero, depending on the state of the river.

For the first forty five minutes we wind along through the rain forest on the River Suete. This runs into the much wider Tortuguero River.

As we continue, we pass Tortuguero Hill, which at one hundred and nineteen metres high is the highest point on the Caribbean coast. There are little jetties along the way, where we drop off supplies for the local communities.

So as we make our way downstream, all eyes are on stalks, on the lookout for wildlife.

We are not disappointed as it does not take long to spot an array of colourful waterfowl, along with caiman and crocodiles.

As we approach our accommodation for the next two nights, it is invisible. All we can see is the jetty surrounded by giant plants.

We are all so excited, we could not get off the boat quick enough.

As we disembarked we were met by our host at the pool with glasses of fresh orange juice.

Wow! We are staying at the Pachira Lodge. Wow! Beautiful.

With keys in hand and suitcases trailing behind us, we walked through the rain forest, looking for our lodge. Our senses are being bombarded by new sights and sounds.

The flora resembles the film set of Avatar, with plants of red, blue, pink, and purple.

The fauna is also very abundant, the list of sightings is

growing. (Watch this space.)

Sylvie's head is in a spin, she doesn't know which way to look. She is looking everywhere but at me, but I can't blame her, this place is amazing.

The lodge is simple but perfect. We even have rocking chairs on the veranda.

For the first time since leaving home, Sylvie is able to unpack. I have packed extra colourful shirts to give the wildlife a run for its money.

After lunch, we head back to the boat to go across to the village of Tortuguero.

Tortuguero is a small village of some 800 inhabitants.
In the area, there are no roads, hence, no cars. Travel is by boat or plane.
On one side of the village are the river and the waterways taking you deep into the jungle. On the other side is the Caribbean beach which welcomes thousands of nesting sea turtles every year
.

The village is on a narrow strip of land between the river and the Caribbean Sea.

We decide to go to the beach.

"Hang on!" exclaims Sylvie, "The beach is black."

Because Costa Rica is a volcanic country, some of the beaches are naturally black. Added to this the waves rolling in are unusually large. Not your typical Caribbean beach.

The beauty of this beach is that every year thousands of sea turtles choose to lay their eggs here. There is now a major conservation programme in place, run by local volunteers to help protect the turtles.

As we walk along the beach and into the village, we spot a man with a wheelbarrow and a machete. In the wheelbarrow are freshly harvested coconuts. Delicious! We later find some in the village with added rum. Dangerous!

From the outside, Tortuguero looks like a shantytown, but as you look deeper, it becomes a quaint, little village with a big personality, with good shops, restaurants and a school.

What it doesn't have are roads, traffic and pollution.

Suddenly there is a commotion up the—I was going to say road, up the lane. Two toucans have landed in a tree and are busy eating the fruit.

As we meet up with the gang, to return to the lodge, we hear reports of an anteater being spotted on the beach. We all muscle in to look at the photographic evidence.

As we go to dinner, we are all in high spirits.

After dinner, the ladies went to do what ladies do. I waited for Sylvie outside the dining room, casually waiting by a tree, where I nearly wet myself.

On our list of wildlife to see are sloths (my choice) and racoons (Sylvie's choice).

So here I am, casually standing by a tree, minding my own business, when two racoons walk pass me and climb up the tree.

Just then, Sylvie turns up. "Sylvie! Sylvie! You've missed them."

"Missed who?"

"Two racoons up the tree," I answer breathlessly.

"Oh! Never mind, perhaps I will see them later. Anyway, some of us are going for a walk with Adonys," she informs me.

Being the sensible one, I'm off for cocktails by the pool with the rest of the gang.

An hour later, the racoons re-appear by the pool, and of course, Sylvie is nowhere to be seen.

"I saw them on our walk," she informs me, "You should have come."

I, of course, was far too busy stressing over racoons.

Anyway, we've had a busy, action-packed day. Time for bed.

When we get back to our lodge, two things strike us.

Number one, the frog chorus has started, with all the local males trying to attract females. The other thing to strike us is the biggest female spider in her web we have ever seen. We know it was a female because in close attendance was a tiny male. (We wonder if he will survive the night.)

Just as my head touches the pillow, it starts to rain. It sounds like marbles hitting a tin roof, which is exactly what we have, in case of volcano eruptions.

We, along with our neighbours take a peek outside. The rain is so heavy, we can't see through it.

Too tired to think about it. Goodnight!

Parque national Tortuguero is a protected wilderness area oh Costa Rica s Northern Caribbean coast. Its beaches are famous as a haven for sea turtles, including the endangered green turtle.

The parks freshwater creeks and lagoons, which can be navigated by boat or canoe, shelter crocodiles, caiman and river turtle.

The surrounding dense rainforest is also rich in wildlife, including monkeys and many bird species.

It covers an area of 312 square kilometres and receives up to 600 centimetres of rain a year.

After breakfast the following morning, we all go for a boat trip along the creeks and canals, and the list of sightings growing by the minute.

Add eaglets, tiger herons, and various waterfowl in an assortment of colours and sizes.

We also spot otters and basilisk lizards (also called the Jesus Christ lizard on account of its ability to run on water), and river turtles.

We were gone for two hours and only explored a minute part of the waterways. There was so much to see, our cameras could not click fast enough.

After lunch, it was time for a bit of downtime by the pool. (Wildlife permitting.)

It doesn't take long for us to hear the cry of green macaws, it's amazing how, although we had only been here a short time, we come to recognise bird calls, and sure enough, moments later a squadron of green macaws come flying overhead.

We then hear reports of spider monkeys in the trees, so off we go to see an acrobatic display put on just for us.

What a magical place!

It's not over yet, around the corner there are hummingbirds vying for our attention.

So much for relaxing by the pool. This place has shown us some awe-inspiring visions of paradise. We think we come from one of the most forward thinking countries in the world, but in some aspects, we are quite backward, especially in looking after our wildlife.

Tomorrow, we move on. Tonight, we had a drink to celebrate.

Chapter Five
Why Did the Banana Cross the Road?

After two days in Tortuguero, it is now time to pack our bags and move on to our next location, which is the Selva Verde lodge in Sarapiquí, an area of chocolate, coffee, pineapples and of course wildlife.

So as we say goodbye to the frog chorus, the giant banana spider residing outside our lodge, with her meal to be, her husband, if he is man enough, we feel that a little piece of us is staying behind.

We make our way back to the boat, stepping over a snake, crossing the path, as if it was the most natural thing in the world.

Seeing the wildlife up close and personal seems natural now, even normal. I guess we have settled into the Costa Rican lifestyle.

So now we have to make our way back upstream to Pavona to meet up with our minibus.

"Who's got the keys?"

On the way to Sarapiquí, we have to pass the aforementioned banana plantations, but there is an obstruction in the road.

In Britain, we sometimes have livestock blocking the road in the countryside. In Costa Rica, they have bananas crossing the road.

To get the bananas from the field to the packing station, they have a conveying system that literally crosses the road.

As mentioned earlier, the bananas are wrapped in blue plastic to keep out spiders. These spiders are poisonous and can kill, which leads me to make a confession.

Many years ago, back in the 70s, I was working at Woolworth. In those days, we sold everything including bananas. So when we got delivery, on one occasion I put a note on the boxes saying, 'DANGER: MAY CONTAIN

SPIDERS,' then stood back as a young female assistant very gingerly opened the boxes and took out the bananas.

For a young man, this was very amusing. Knowing what I know now I wish to apologise to her.

Banana cultivation started in 1878. Costa Rica was the first Central American nation to plant bananas.

In 1880, the Atlantic railway was completed, which helped the development of the banana export.

This brought in outside investment, which in turn, made banana growing, big business.

In 1911, Costa Rica became the largest producers of bananas, and despite problems with the labour force, diseases and pollution, business is still blooming.

In Costa Rica, the wildlife has priority. So if you find a crocodile taking up residence in the grounds of your accommodation, well, that's okay, it's quite normal. If you leave him alone, he won't bother you. Pura vida.

If you spend enough time in the rainforest, with the wildlife and fast flowing rivers, then you are bound to come across, or even go across a dodgy looking bridge.

The bridge in question crosses the Sarapiquí River, a fast flowing river, used for white water rafting. We, the gang, decided to cross the dodgy looking bridge, but for safety, we'll go three at a time. There was no particular reason to cross this bridge, other than because it was there, and we are on an adventure holiday.

Our accommodation at Selva Verde was similar to that at Tortuguero, except for two things our lodge was built on stilts, as a precaution against flooding. The other difference was, as well as rocking chairs on the veranda, there was also a hammock (if only we had time to enjoy these comforts).

We were here for one night only. No need for Sylvie to unpack.

At breakfast the following morning, there was a commotion outside. Upon investigation, we found a table laden with bananas, being fought over by a flock of birds of the toucan family.

Today, we are going on a guided walk on the other side of the river, which means crossing THAT bridge again.

Then we are back on the road.

Chapter Six
Volcanoes and Waterfalls

On the drive from Sarapiquí to La Fortuna, our next port of call, we were promised a treat.

The journey itself was quite pleasant, with rolling hills, to remind us of home, but we're in Costa Rica. To drive home the point, we pass coffee plantations, monkeys watching us from the trees, cattle egrets in the fields, and vultures circling in the sky overhead.

After a couple of hours, we stopped in a small town for an ice-cream break, what a treat!

Hang on a minute, what's that outside the ice-cream parlour. Two giant iguanas measuring over five foot from nose to tail, sunbathing.

They seem to be quite tame, even approachable, some of the gang feel that they could stroke them.

There some more around the corner. It's a strange sight-seeing these monsters in the trees.

Sylvie notices that some of them are bright orange.

Have they been in a tanning booth? We are told that these are males ready for the mating game. Ten out of ten for effort.

As we continue our journey, we are the lookout for Mount Arenal, the active volcano.

The Arenal volcano is the highest, and most active in the country.

The last major eruption was in 1968, which buried three small villages and left 87 people dead. Since then eruptions have been constant, though much less severe.

Since 2010, Arenal has been sleeping.

If you ask a child to draw a volcano, they would probably get it about right. The volcano is a perfect cone shape, if we could only see it. On our visit, it was shrouded in a low rain cloud and just refused to come out to play.

When you have a British seaside holiday, the in-car game is to be the first to spot the sea. In La Fortuna, the game is to spot the volcano.

La Fortuna is a sleepy little town. Although it is a quiet town, it is all geared up for the tourists, with organised trips, restaurants, souvenir shops, and most importantly, there are banks.

After three days in the rainforest, it was nice to see civilisation again. As we make our way to our hotel, we pass many hotels advertising hot springs.

Our guide Adonys, informs us that these are usually very busy and that he had something special lined up for us. We know him well enough to trust him. So we drive on.

We arrived at our hotel, Los Lagos, just in time for lunch, but not before Sylvie has unpacked.

For lunch, we have gallo pinto, which we learnt, is the name given to black beans and rice.

After lunch we have a bit of free time, so we decide to explore the hotel grounds the first thing we see is a frog. Big, green, and plastic.

Sylvie can't get enough of the wildlife, so we head off to the animal sanctuary.

We find the turtles, sleeping, and the crocodiles sunbathing, open-mouthed. (Why is it, that animals in captivity are like lifeless dummies, and those in the wild are hyperactive?) We are already missing the rainforest.

Further on, we found the butterfly house, where the inmates are busy gorging themselves on rotting fruit.

We then come across a colony of leaf-cutter ants carrying relatively enormous pieces of leaf to nowhere in particular.

Anyway, time for some relaxation. On the hill, there is a series of pools heated by hot springs. So we made our way to the lowest pool, which, by chance, has a bar. Time for a cocktail or two.

The following morning, after breakfast, we took a 15-minute drive to see the waterfalls. This involved a 20-minute descent to the river where we, the gang, decided to go for a swim, (the water was surprisingly warm).

On the climb back up, we stop for photos and witness the birth of a new waterfall. A once in a lifetime treat.

Before lunch, we have time to visit La Fortuna town

centre, to buy some much-needed souvenirs, once we were able to use the bank's hole in the wall. I know this sounds ordinary, but we haven't seen these things since we left San

José, I don't know how many days ago. It is very easy to lose track of time when it is not important.

We have already had a dip in the river, under the waterfalls. Now it was time to visit the hot springs, but not just any hot springs that we passed in the various hotels on route.

We arrived at the Tabacón Hot Springs. It was so exclusive, we had the place to ourselves until a group of Canadians arrived. We didn't mind though. We were so relaxed by the experience, we were happy to share. Bonus points to our guide for bringing us to one of the best spas in the world.

There were three spa pools, on three levels, varying in temperature, in glorious surroundings.

It has to be one of the world's best luxuries, drinking cocktails, (mine was a bbc—banana, Baileys and coconut—dangerous), in a thermal pool surrounded by tropical rain forest.

As an added bonus, we were able to enjoy dinner in the restaurants, which was very pleasant.

Sylvie was so relaxed, she didn't mind packing again.

The following morning, Juan, our driver is missing. He didn't come to breakfast. It's okay, we are told he had gone on ahead with our minibus.

We would meet up with him on the other side of Lake Arenal. We were going to cross the lake by boat, on our way to Monteverde, our next destination.

Chapter Seven
Flying High

Lake Arenal is Costa Rica's largest landlocked body of water, with a surface area of nearly 33 square miles, with a depth of up to 200 feet.

The lake is surrounded by rolling hills of pasture ground and forest, while the Arenal volcano dominates the eastern horizon.

In 1979, Lake Arenal was enlarged to three times its original size with the construction of the hydroelectric dam, which meant that the town of Arenal had to be moved.

The old town of Arenal and that of Tronadora now lies at the bottom of the lake.

To get across the lake we took the waterbus, which was run by a husband and wife team. Today, the wife was taking the lead, but as we got halfway across, the wind picked up, and the lake got quite rough, enough for the husband to take over.

For us, it was quite exhilarating as we were passing islands on the lake, although thought provoking when you realise these aren't islands but hilltops.

On the other side of the lake, we were met by Juan and our trusty minibus, and we continued our drive to Monteverde.

This part of the country reminded us of North Wales, in particular, Snowdonia, with its narrow, twisting roads in amongst the rolling hills.

In Monteverde, we were staying for two nights, (so Sylvie can unpack again), at the four star Establo Mountain Hotel, which was built by the Quakers, on the edge of the rainforest.

The small Quaker community in Costa Rica was founded in 1951 by a group of 11 families from Alabama. Four young friends had recently been jailed for refusing to serve in the Korean war, so the families were looking for somewhere they could live in peace. They chose Costa Rica because there is no army.

This hotel had the wow factor in one direction the view is of the rainforest, in the other direction, there are rolling hills leading to the Gulf of Nicoya off the Pacific Ocean.

Our room was on the ground floor, and the view was so wonderful I felt compelled to go outside with my camera, whereas Sylvie said she was more compelled to take a bath.

For her own peace of mind, she decides to close the French windows. So now I was locked out.

"I can't open the door," she shouts, after eventually coming to my rescue.

"What do mean, you can't open the door?" I shouted through the glass.

"I don't know how to release the catch," replied Sylvie.

"You will have to get some help," I tell her.

Just then a porter arrives with our luggage and comes to my rescue. My hero.

"Shall we go to dinner?"

Although we are staying in a four-star hotel in beautiful surroundings, this is Costa Rica and the wildlife is never far away.

We got a reminder the following morning. On our way to breakfast, we became aware that there was an animal ahead of us. Instead of cautiously keeping our distance, we fearlessly, if not stupidly tried to catch up with it. I don't know what we would have done if it had been dangerous.

It turned out to be harmless, if hungry, white-nosed coati, (related to the racoon), looking for his breakfast.

Up to this point, on this adventure holiday, we have been spectators, now it was time to take part in the great adventure.

The gang were split into two groups. One group went with Super Sylvie for a skywalk through the Monteverde rainforest along walking trails and 8 suspension bridges, up to 170 metres in length, and up to 60 metres above the ground.

I call Sylvie Super because she walked along these bridges, even though she has a major fear of heights, and she enjoyed the experience. Bravo, Sylvie!

Meanwhile, I was with the other group, doing the canopy tour along zip wires.

We were led away into the tackle room, where we were trussed up like chickens in our safety harnesses. You also get the option to rent a camera for your helmet. We were advised not to bother as we would not appear on the subsequence film, but on second thought, I wish I had.

Before we started, we needed a safety briefing. This took place in an area where they filmed the new *Paddington Bear* film. Then we were ready to travel through the rainforest, going along 15 zip wires.

The first wire was quite short. I guess this was to get us used to the experience and to pull out if necessary. Then they steadily got longer and higher.

You get an enormous sense of freedom as you 'fly' high above the canopy, and observe the extent of the rainforest.

It was so humbling, as you feel so small in the grand scheme of things.

By the time I arrived at the last wire, it was raining quite heavily. The last was also the longest, so long that you could not see the end, it was lost in the cloud.

Being the longest wire, it took 53 seconds to get to the end, and travelling upside down, with my face to the rain. When I got to the end, my face was numb with cold.

It was such an amazing experience. I thought I was being quite macho, with my hardhat and leather gloves, flying through the rainforest canopy, attached to a length of wire. That was until I found out that directly behind were two ten-year-old American girls. They were so macho.

When you get to the last tower you are given the option to go on the 'Tarzan swing'. You get attached to a rope 15 metres above, and when told, you jump from the platform.

I jumped the gun and the guys at the bottom weren't ready. Everyone was rolling about with laughter as the safetyman struggled to catch my rope. I found the whole experience frighteningly exhilarating, and in the end, I was laughing hysterically.

I later met up with Sylvie in the more sedate world of hummingbirds, where we shared our experiences.

When we got back to our hotel, we were informed that 250 Americans have just arrived, so our dinner was going to be earlier than planned. We did not mind, it gave us more time in the bar.

Chapter Eight
Riding the Ponies and Riding the Rapids

We're on the road again, making our way to our last stopover, the Hotel Hacienda Guachipelin, on the edge of the Rincon de la Vieja national park.

A lot of our travel is on the Pan American Highway, which looks enormous, compared with the mountain roads we had travelled on.

We pass through some non-tourist towns including Juntas, which although looking like a sleepy town was anything but during the years of the gold fever.

As we entered the gateway to the hotel it was like going to a ranch. Our room was in the style of a bungalow, and we had a mango tree outside our room.

Looking around we see a stable yard full of horses, reminding us that our adventure is not over. Both Sylvie and I have ridden before, never at home, but we have been horse riding in Spain and Turkey. Now we are adding Costa Rica to the top of our list, wow!

The horsemen look us up and down and put us with the right horse, and you just bond with them. We then had a very pleasant ride through the countryside for a couple of hours.

The horses know the routine so well; they know exactly where to go, to the point that if you try to guide them offline they rebel. So the best thing to do is sit still and let your horse take you for a ride, and just enjoy the view.

Part two was a wake-up call. We were going tubing in a fast flowing river with rapids.

When I say tubing, I mean a rubber ring about the size of a tractor wheel going down a river full of rocks. Are we mad or what?

This involved putting on a safety helmet and going for a long walk, carrying your rubber ring as best as you can.

Sylvie had the best idea, the ring being bigger than her, she found a young man to carry it for her.

We had no idea where the river was, we just followed the human chain until we eventually heard the river.

We still could not see the river, but it sounded terrifying.

We all looked at each other as we thought, *what have we done?*

When we reached the river, it was not as bad as we thought; you needed some movement so that we could go downstream. So the start was quite pleasant. Then we hit our first set of rapids, now we knew why we were wearing safety helmets.

Not in case you hit head on the rocks, but as you reach the rapids, you get caught up in a vortex, and as you get in a spin you are in danger of kicking someone in the head or even being kicked yourself.

As we headed down the river, it getting faster, and the rapids were getting steeper, and we were bouncing off the boulders. Ouch!

At long last, we reached the end of our run, time to leave the river if you could.

Sylvie, along with some of the other ladies found this a struggle. Trying to get her ring out of the water she fell in, I guess she was enjoying herself so much she didn't want to leave.

On reflection, not our favourite experience, and quite painful when your backside makes contact with a rock.

The evening was our last together as the gang, before making our separate ways home, so it was time for farewell cocktails and email address exchange.

Chapter Nine
Homeward Bound

Breakfast was a quiet affair. Today we were all going our separate ways, some going to the airport and some moving on to all-inclusive beach hotels for a few days.

Sylvie and I were going to the airport, but our flight wasn't until the following day.

So two by two, we left our minibus and said goodbye to our shrinking gang, and giving a big adios to Adonys and Juan. It was the end of our big adventure.

Our last stop was at the Hilton Garden Inn. We had given ourselves the option of going to the beach, which was a few miles away. The hotel would have organised the trip for us, but when we saw the outdoor pool we decided to spend the day chillaxing (a term I picked up from the singer Adele) and catching up with our reading.

It was probably the hottest day of our visit. We had to keep going into the pool to cool down. Nice!

When it got too hot, Sylvie went to explore the hotel shop.

It was probably the best shop in Costa Rica, and where we brought our souvenirs.

Our room at the Hilton Garden Inn was enormous, you could get lost in it, reminding us of the Grand Hotel in Toronto, (that's another story).

Then it got to the time for our last dinner. I, of course, had to finish with rice and black beans, and Sylvie had the salad of course.

The following morning, all packed up it was time to say goodbye to Costa Rica and make our way to the airport for our long flight home, via Houston.

Houston, we're going home.

It's All French to Me

Chapter 1
Going North to Brittany

We had already been to Costa Rica and the Algarve this year, so the question was 'where to next?'

I have always had a soft spot for Yorkshire. My family come from York. I last went to Yorkshire nearly 40 years ago, when I went to Leeds, Harrogate and Knaresborough. A friend of ours had moved to Halifax a year ago, so we had an open invitation to visit whenever. So, to me, this seemed to be the prime opportunity to go to Yorkshire.

"How do you fancy Brittany?" asked Sylvie, one day. Not somewhere I had in mind, to be honest, not exactly Scarborough or Hebden Bridge, but okay.

We had previously been to France three times. We went to Paris for our honeymoon. While in Sussex, we went to Boulounge for a day trip. Our third visit was back to Paris, as I was running in the Paris marathon. Sylvie knows the Paris metro system better than the London underground.

So, where in Brittany were we to go. Brittany is similar in size to Devon and Cornwall and is very much alike in topography. It would be like home with an accent.

We decided to do an independent tour, but not with the car, we would use the French transport system. So out came the map and the internet.

The route we chose was Portsmouth, St Malo, Dinan, Bénodet, Roscoff and Plymouth.

The preferred transport was Cross Channel Ferry, train and riverboat. Organising the ferry was straightforward enough, booking French trains surprisingly easy, the riverboats not so. The website seems old and out of date and in French. We'll check them out when we get there. Booking seats for the trains in England was much more difficult.

If you get tickets from the railway station it's okay, but there is just the one price, the expensive, no options. To check the timetable and ticket prices we use the train line website, the only drawback is that it is a race against time if you are not quick enough the website closes and you have to start again, but if you persevere there are bargains to be had. After several attempts, seats are booked.

Packed and ready, let's go. Newton Abbot to Exeter, change. Exeter to Salisbury, change. Salisbury to Portsmouth Harbour. So far so good, just the one snag. Whenever we book seats on the train we always choose forward facing seats and every time without fail we are given rear facing, why do we bother?

When we got to the station at Portsmouth Harbour, we play the game 'spot the harbour'. We ended up getting a taxi. Good job too as it would have been quite a hike.

The Brittany Ferries departure area was surprisingly quiet, with very few foot passengers going through. A glance out of the window explains the reason. There is a massively long line of lorries, cars, and campervans waiting to board.

This was going to be a 12-hour crossing starting at 8 p.m. A micro cruise. We had even booked a cabin for the night, we did not fancy sitting in a bucket seat all night, we much preferred getting to St Malo refreshed.

As we board the Armorique, we were greeted with a "Bonsoir monsieur et madame." Here we go, how's our French?

We made our way to our cabin, compact but perfectly adequate for our needs, then made our way to one of the dining rooms for our evening meal, which for us was surprisingly good, washed down with a glass of wine. After dinner, it was time to explore the rest of the ship. We went on deck to view the Portsmouth skyline, (we will have to return to see Portsmouth properly).

We made our way to the show area as two young ladies were in the middle of their magic act. We stayed for a drink, the ladies were followed by a cabaret singer. All in all, a good evening. Time for bed.

Sleeping arrangement consists of two bunk beds, Sylvie on the bottom, me on the top. I noticed there was a safety belt attached to my bed. Is that to keep me in bed during rough seas?

After a good night's sleep, awoke refreshed and ready to take on the French language and so we went for breakfast before disembarking in St Malo.

Chapter 2
St Malo

As we exited the port of St Malo, we could see the walled old town, looking imposing and impregnable. It wasn't far so we decided to walk to the hotel. The Hotel Les Ajoncs d'Or.

As we arrived early in the morning, our room was not ready (guests were still having breakfast). The staff were good enough to store our luggage in a back room, while we explored the town.

We started by looking at the shops and restaurants, I found myself walking sideways as we walked past the patisserie. In the end, Sylvie had to drag me away, through one of the arched gateways.

Beyond the wall and a beach is a countless number of islands and islets.

We decided that the best way to get an overview of the area was to walk along the fortifications around the town, so we climbed the steps on the north wall and walked in a clockwise direction.

To the east was the new town of St Malo, to the south was the harbour and the River Rance, to the west there was a myriad of islands, and to the north was a seascape dominated by an island with a fort perched on the top.

These all needed investigating.

As we made our way around, we spotted a riverside office selling boat tickets.

The plan was to go up the River Rance to Dinan, our next destination. So we made our way to the office on the riverbank.

The office was closed, but there was a sign informing us that the boat to Dinan goes once a week, on Saturdays, today is Sunday. We are going to have to be flexible and make other arrangements for tomorrow.

We made our way to the tourist information centre. Time for a bit more practice of my French, (I am finding that the more I use it the more fluent I am getting, to the point that people actually understand the words I am using.)

The result was that there are trains going to Dinan on the Monday, itinerary back on track. Let's get back to our walk on the city wall.

As we made our way along the west wall we saw so many islands and rocks, we decided that to navigate these waters you would need to be a very skilled sailor.

While we were admiring the view, we noticed that the tide was receding and a causeway was being exposed. Time for a boiled egg sandwich as our glamorous picnic lunch.

Meanwhile, the tide had receded sufficiently, that we could walk across to the island. It was a very small island, it only took 20 minutes to get around it. Our reason for going to the island? It was there. We found out that the name of the island is Le Petit Bé.

From the other side of the island, we could see people walking to a neighbouring island, Le Grand Bé. We did not want to press our luck; we, I mean Sylvie, has a history with causeways and islands, so we made our way back to the mainland. Phew! We made it in one piece.

Back on the wall, we make our way along the north, from where we saw a much larger island with a fort in the centre, the Fort National. This definitely needed more investigation so another causeway, this time with a barrier of rocks and boulders.

"Just take it easy, Sylvie."

On this island, there was a small charge and a group of tour guides to take you around, but we're on an independent holiday, so we strolled around independently. When we reached the summit of the island we got a magnificent panoramic view of the area.

We discovered that the fort here and the ones on Le Petit Bé, and Le Grand Bé were built at the end of the 17th century to keep out the English and Dutch fleet, whilst keeping the royally connected pirates safe.

With the sea, the islands and rocks, the walled city, the place looks impregnable.

As we left the island, dodging the rocks and boulders, and made it back to the mainland we felt the need to celebrate. Sylvie had a cup of tea, I had a glass of cidre, (it was French). Let me explain.

We live In South Devon, a beautiful part of the country, with rolling hills and glorious beaches.

One day we took a drive to Bigbury. From there, at low tide, you can walk across a causeway to Burgh Island (as used by Agatha Christie in many of her novels. Did you know she lived here in South Devon?) with its famous Pilchard Inn.

When the time to leave the island arrived, the tide was coming in, but not to worry because there was a tractor to take us across the causeway.

We arrived at the tractor, climbed on board then saw the notice, 'If the tractor is unattended do not board'. So off we got and waited. Sylvie then decided to explore the rock pools.

Suddenly, I heard a yelp of pain, Sylvie had slipped on the rocks and twisted her ankle. She then had to be carried onto the tractor.

I managed to get Sylvie to the car, but she could not drive, and I don't drive. We were stuck. Mobile reception was non-existent, but there was a call box up the road, so I telephoned Sylvie's parents.

They never found us, and we waited, and waited, but nothing, the area was getting deserted so that in the end, we had to get an ambulance, which took an hour to get us to Torbay hospital.

Once there we discovered that she had in fact broken her ankle, and had to have pins inserted. (Great fun at airports.) We have never been back since.

Anyway, Sylvie has finished her tea, I've drunk my cider. (I'm not really a cider drinker, but when in cider country...). Actually, it was very good.

It's time to get back to the hotel as we haven't booked in yet. The people at the hotel are very friendly and there was no problem.

The bigger problem, no matter where we are, is where to go and what to eat, especially as Sylvie is a vegetarian.

In Brittany, the staple diet is fish and shellfish. Sylvie doesn't eat fish. The alternative is galettes, whatever they are.

So we spent the evening perusing the menus, trying to find something we might recognise. We even passed an Afghan restaurant, that was surprisingly very quiet, (no diners).

Anyway, we found a nice little French looking place. On the menu, galettes, which turned out to be a squared shaped savoury pancake. Of course, I had to wash it down with cider, but what's this? My cider was served in a bowl! As a consequence, I now drink from a bowl and the dog drinks from a glass.

The following morning we were to go to Dinan, but how were we to get there.

We were told to take the number two bus to the train station. I don't know if we looked lost, or that we weren't welcome, but everyone was falling over themselves to help us find a train. The train was modem, clean, and on time, a world away from British Rail.

We had to change trains at Dol de Bretagne, and because we had to wait a while for our connection, we took a stroll into the town centre, and wow! What fantastic buildings, very old and very beautiful. We were so pleased to have stopped here. An architect's dream, with a promise of more to come when we get to Dinan.

Chapter 3
Dinan

When we arrived at Dinan, the first thing to strike us was the size of the railway station. In France, they are relatively small. Dinan was no exception, but it was a pretty station with its hand-drawn plan of the town on the wall.

As we left the station, we turned left and followed the signs for the old town.

It did not take long to reach the outer wall of the old town, but how do you get beyond the wall? Out came the map. We found the route and were just walking off when we heard this middle-aged woman shouting at us. I had left my camera on a post whilst looking at my map. I was very grateful but did not understand a word she was saying. The more excited the French get, the faster they speak. I wish me well.

Five minutes later, we hit the medieval old town with some of its buildings dating back to the 13th century. Wow! No matter how much research you do, nothing can prepare you for the sight before you.

Living in South Devon, we quite often go to Dartmouth (the set for the original series of *Poldark*) which has a few 17th-century buildings, but these pale into insignificance compared to Dinan. It is like the scene for the film *Timeline* starring Billy Connelly (check it out).

If you are going to be in Dinan for any length of time then you need to stay in the old town. We stayed at the Hôtel de la Tour de l'Horloge, which was located behind the clock tower.

We headed for the clock tower hoping to see the hotel, and after much to-in and froing, we eventually found it down a side street.

The hotel was small and quirky, with the reception on the first floor. We were given room two, and upon entering we were transported to French Morocco, it could have been Rick's place in Casablanca. It was beautiful.

We are not ones for hanging around hotels, so it does not take us long to hit the tourist trail.

The first place to go was the Rue du Jerzual, one of the oldest thoroughfares in Dinan. It is the main road from the river to the town, and in the past would have been a very busy and vibrant part of town.

Now it is a very steep cobbled street, full of tourist with cameras around their necks, including Sylvie and myself. At the bottom of the road is the River Rance, with its riverside cafés and bars. (This was where we were hoping to land by boat from St Malo.) Straddling the river is the most elegant viaduct, and on the river, there are boats that do trips upstream.

"Let's go and see if we can do a trip," suggests Sylvie. We could not see anyone who might be able to help us, so we decided that it might be an idea to go to the tourist information centre.

So back we went up to the Rue du Jerzual.

"Cor! Look at all these tourists, keep moving, Sylvie, they'll take a photo of anything stationary." She just gave me a knowing look, you know, the one that says 'harks who's talking'. I don't know what she meant.

Anyway, we made our way back through the old town, (isn't it surprising how, the more time you spend in a place, the smaller it gets?). It didn't take us long to get to the other side of town, and then, one more step, and we transported back to present day Dinan, with banks, shops and a tourist information centre.

After purchasing our boat tickets, we returned to medieval Dinan in time for dinner.

So here we go on the vegetarian merry go round. In France, they seem to eat a lot of fish and meat, but we found a place we liked.

After dinner, the town became very quiet, so we retired to our room to watch French TV and brush up on my French.

As we settled down, we found that our room was the centre of the universe, with everyone walking, nosily past our room. (Our tiny hotel has turned into a 400-room monster) but being British, we didn't complain.

Up with the larks the following morning, we started the day with a continental breakfast. Our stomachs are too old to deal with a full English. We had a full day planned, so we needed to crack on.

First on the agenda was a walk along the ramparts. We started to the west of the town, but it was quite difficult finding our way along the wall, as there were many false starts. Once we got to the castle we were on our way, and we enjoyed many fine views inside, looking at the historical centre, and outside, with views of the countryside.

Time for a coffee.

Next stop, La Tour de l'Horloge. The clock tower. As you climb the stairs, you pass rooms filled with historical artefacts, and as you reach the attic, you can go out onto the roof, and admire the vistas, très bien.

We haven't got time to go all French, we have to grab a bite and make our way back down to the river, we have a boat to catch don't you know.

This reminds me of the last time we were on a boat in France. We were on a bateaux mouche in Paris, during our honeymoon. It was freezing.

Today, the weather is very pleasant, much more like it, and we had a very nice little cruise upstream.

When we returned, we just had enough time to scan the shops, before our nightly gastro struggle. Around here, people seem to retire early, so we made our way to modem day Dinan, and settle for a pizza.

Chapter 4
By the Seaside at Bénodet

The following morning it was time to say goodbye to Dinan as we progressed on our tour. Next stop, Bénodet via Quimper, so it was back on the train for another trip through the French countryside.

At Quimper, the train terminates, so we had to make alternative travel plans. Outside the station, was the bus terminus, where I managed, with my best French, to secure two tickets on the bus to Bénodet.

The trouble with independent travel is that you don't know when you need to get off the bus. As we passed through Bénodet, we did see one or two shops, but not what I would call a town centre, so we stayed put on the bus hoping that the bus would take us to the centre.

"We are now leaving Bénodet," the driver shouted to us. Oh!

Right, we had better get off.

"We are staying at the Hotel Ker Vennaik," I inform the driver as if he was our tour guide.

"It is on the right hand road," he says, with his finger pointing in the general direction.

"Merci beaucoup," I thank him. (Incidentally, I had noticed that the French school children were very polite when leaving the bus. "Merci monsieur," they would all say.)

Anyway, the road we were directed to was the right one. It was just, unfortunately, the longest road in France, and the hotel was situated at the other end. We were so relieved to have found it.

We got past the flirty receptionist and found our room. Very pleasant. Time to explore.

We found the beach, very nice, with great views. We found the river, beautiful, with riverboats, interesting. We found the church and a couple of tourist shops, closed; but where was the town centre, there was not one, just a couple of shops on a side street, closed.

"What are we going to eat?" I asked feeling quite ravenous.

We found a couple of restaurants and hotels, but they were not Sylvie-friendly. We did find a pizza parlour that was okay, but on closer inspection was quite grubby, we did not go there again.

The following morning, after a hearty breakfast, we were ready to explore, and the shops were open.

We found there was a waiting boat docked, that was doing a cruise up the River Odet, so we quickly purchased tickets and jumped on board.

The Odet is considered one of the prettiest rivers in France. As we sat, with a hot drink in hand, watching the French countryside drift by we were in no mood to disagree. It was indeed a beautiful river.

On each side of the river are woods, fields and fabulous chateaus. After a while, the town of Quimper comes into view, just as we turn around and head downstream, back toward Bénodet and beyond as we skirt around the islands in the bay.

After a quick spot of lunch, we met the bus that would take us back to Quimper.

Shops, we have shops, lots of shops. And beautiful buildings and shops, and museums and shops, and restaurants and shops. It's a beautiful town, Quimper.

With so many places to eat, we indulged before going back to our hotel.

The following morning, we were back on the road to our final destination Roscoff.

Chapter 5
Royal Roscoff

The original plan was to go from Bénodet to Quimper by boat and from Quimper to Roscoff by train.

In reality, we went from Bénodet to Quimper by bus, from Quimper to Morlaix by train, and Morlaix to Roscoff by bus.

When we arrived at Roscoff railway station, we could immediately understand why there was no train. The station looked as if it had been bombed during the war, and was still awaiting restoration.

Our present problem, which way to the town centre?

After going around the houses, literally, Sylvie eventually put us on the right road, and we enjoyed the walk along the seafront to the old town.

We were booked into the Grand Hotel de la Mer, as grand as its name, with the most enormous window in the dining room, with the most breathtaking view of the sea. We were ready to move in, but history was waiting.

All we knew about Roscoff was this is a ferry port, the gateway to France, but there was so much more, we were walking through history. Mary, Queen of Scots stayed here in the 16th century, and there are plaques all over the town full of historical facts.

Sylvie is the history buff, while I am still trying to get past 1066, but I'm learning. Walking through history makes more interesting and educational. (Bring the kids)

On our return to the hotel, we had a visitor, sitting outside our window was a parrot, as tame as you like. When I opened the window ajar it was ready to fly in. I guess it was being fed by the previous guest.

The following morning I awoke to the most stunning sunrise, so I was out with camera quicker than you could say bonj… The sunrise was the most dazzling I have ever seen, before or since.

After breakfast, we had a stroll around the harbour before catching the ferry to Plymouth and home.

Chapter 1
We Are Sailing...

Having enjoyed our 'mini cruise' to France, our minds turned to the full-length version. Our 20th wedding anniversary would be next year in 2018, so we thought now would be a good time to give ourselves a trial run.

We chose a cruise around the Canary Islands and Madeira, as we were looking to go in March, with the plan that if enjoyed the experience, we would celebrate our 20th anniversary in the Caribbean.

With the experience of innocence, we chose our cruise company and destination we booked and paid our deposit. Then came the extras.

We wanted to be sure to have a cabin with a window and a double bed, so I chose cabin 442. The price now started to rise.

Sylvie thought it would be a good idea to go on a tour at each port of call. The price continues to rise.

My next idea was to buy a drinks package. Our meals were already paid for, as we did not want a shock when we got our bill, (cocktails in comfort). Up goes the cost.

"Why don't we have a couple of days in Tenerife at the end of the cruise?" enquires Sylvie. So we booked a three-day extension in Puerto de la Cruz, which raised two points. Isn't innocence experience expensive? And who's paying for all these extras?

We found that getting advance train tickets was actually cheaper than driving and parking at the airport.

Hurray! We've saved money. Then we spoiled it all by booking an airport hotel. We chose the unforgettable Airport Inn, pre-cruise and on the return journey. Now the cost has more than doubled.

Why stop there? As I mentioned, it was to be our anniversary, so I added the celebration package. Surely, this must be the end of our innocent madness.

So at last, the day arrived. Work completed, and put out of minds, we had time to loiter. Our train was booked for five forty-one, so we spent the day completing our packing, (making sure that we were not over the weight limit). We spent the rest of the day charging mobile phones, iPad and cameras. We did last minute checks on the weather forecast for the Canary Islands. Generally pottering around, clock watching until at last, it was time to make our way to the railway station.

Let the adventure begin. Is it too late to check our passports?

The train journey started out pleasant enough, as we sat back in our pre-booked seats. Then out came Sylvie's competitive side.

We had both brought along two novels for those quieter moments. So while I was happy to just sit back and contemplate our voyage, Sylvie was making a start on book one, asking me the loaded question, "Are you not starting a book yet?"

I refused to be drawn into this game, so continued to watch the dusk fall, until, the only thing I could see through the window was our reflection.

There was Sylvie serenely reading her book, while I was sitting there gnashing my teeth. Well, if you can't beat her, you might as well join her, so out came book one.

We were still reading when the train pulled into Reading, where we had to change trains. The plan was to get a drink between connections. If only we the time. Our onward train was already in, waiting for us. "Come on, Sylvie."

A little over an hour later and we arrived at Gatwick Airport, where we spent half an hour looking for a taxi. Yes, I know they are just outside but remember we come from sleepy Devon.

Once boarded we made our way to our hotel, tired and hungry.

We got to the hotel at ten thirty, checked in and picked up our keys. This was when we got the earth-shattering news that the restaurant closed at ten o'clock. Not to worry, there was a petrol station around the corner, where we could get a sandwich, and there were tea-making facilities in our room.

No problem, we thought, until we got to the said petrol station. Not only was the door closed, but it was also locked.

Fortunately, there was a service hatch that was open for business.

"Good evening, we would like a sandwich please." was my opening gambit.

"What sort of sandwich would you like?" challenged the assistant.

"I don't know, what have you got?" I responded, raising the stakes.

Silence.

"Do you have egg and cress?" asked Sylvie in a vain attempt to bring some sensibleness into the conversation.

So off he went to the chill cabinet, returning with an armful of sandwiches.

"I'll take the egg mayo," said Sylvie.

"And I'll have the cheese salad. Oh! Can we have two KitKats as well please?"

He was not amused as he trudged off. He then stopped suddenly, mid-stride.

"Is there anything else I can get you?" he asked, fearing another walk around the shelves.

"I'm going to need a bottle of water please."

"Oh, Sylvie! You are pushing our luck."

Armed with our supper, we raced back to the hotel, took the lift to the fourth floor, found our room and, nothing.

The key would not work. We could not get into our room.

So off I went, back in the lift, down to reception, got our key recharged, back into the lift, up to the fourth floor, found Sylvie waiting patiently. Success, we were in. Put the kettle on.

The following morning, we planned to have a decent breakfast. So having repacked our toiletries, we left our cases in our room, while we went down to the dining room and tucked in.

Having eaten and drunk to our satisfaction, we returned to our room to collect our cases.

"Oh no, Sylvie! Here we go again."

No matter how many attempts I made, we could not get in. So back down to reception I went.

The receptionist was not amused.

"You've worn out the magnet," she informed me as she handed me a replacement, without the faintest flicker of a smile.

Back up to the fourth floor in double quick time, only without success, the door was not budging.

"Now what? I'm not going back to reception."

Just then, a cleaner came around the corner and she had a master key. We quickly grabbed our cases and scampered out of the hotel, to wait in the cold to be picked up by the airport transfer bus.

How many people can you get on a bus with luggage?

We lost count, we only knew we were jammed in like sardines. Breathe in, Sylvie. We made it to the North Terminal, where we all tumbled off the bus.

Having gone through check-in we made our way to the departure lounge. During this process, there was a need to remain focused, as we followed the 'yellow brick road' through the duty-free shop. Eyes straight ahead, we got through without parting with any cash.

When going to any airport we always have must buys.

For me, this includes travel mags. For Sylvie, it's sweets and travel sickness tablets of a certain size, and of course, a bottle of water.

Anyway, we got the call, time to go to the departure gate. I don't know why we always feel the need to rush to the gate.

"Gangway! Coming through!" Our seats on the plane have been pre-booked, so I don't know the reason for the panic. Will they take off without us?

Take off. Destination Tenerife.

Chapter 2
On the Open Seas

After an eventless flight, (there is only so much excitement you can take) we landed at Tenerife South Airport. The sun was shining, the air was warm. We collected our luggage and made our way to a waiting coach, for the next stage, a 45-minute journey to our ship, but we can't relax too much as we are handed an envelope of information and instructions.

"Hold on! Stop the bus! Where is my mobile phone?"

I had left it on the plane, but I was reassured that it would probably be taken to lost property, so I was not overly concerned. I am one of those people who does not like personal technology. I like to escape so that no one can contact me 24/7, so I'll pick it up later on the way home. I still had my iPad so I wasn't a total recluse.

"Ship ahoy!" There she was, our home for the next seven days, the Thomson Majesty.

Before we could board the ship, we had to go through certain formalities. We were given new luggage labels to attach to our cases so that they could be delivered to our cabin. We were also given boarding passes that also served as cabin keys. I hope these work okay.

Next, we had a hand washing ceremony. Because of the fear of norovirus, we were to spend the whole cruise washing our hands, which is not a bad thing when there are over a thousand people on board.

Now the excitement really got to us as we walked on the gangway into the heart of the ship.

At this point, I was feeling a little nervous. You see I had chosen and booked our cabin, it had to have a window and a double bed. When we entered our cabin, it was perfect.

Small but perfectly formed.

Because it was our wedding anniversary, in our cabin, waiting for us was a bunch of flowers, a bottle of champagne and a plate of chocolate-covered strawberries. (Do I get bonus points for arranging this?)

So there we are taking in our surroundings, unpacking our cases when we get a wake-up call.

Suddenly we got an announcement come through our sound system, letting us know that, in a few minutes we were to have a practise, how to abandon ship.

Five minutes later, we heard seven whistles, (we counted them) and one long blast, so we grab our life jacket and made our way to the muster station.

You know how it is when you have a fire drill at work, annoying, and we've all experienced the safety briefing on a flight. On board ship, trussed up in your life jacket, it suddenly feels very real, and in your mind, you can hear Céline Dion singing *My heart will go on*. Anyway, the drill comes to an end and we put our life jackets back into the wardrobe, hoping we will never see them again. I need a drink!

By now, you have probably noticed that we are very good at doing our homework, Sylvie has organised our excursions at each port of call. My job was to commit to memory the layout of the ship. Now was the time to put me to the test.

It was time for dinner and we both were ravenous, and as it was our first evening, we headed for the buffet dining room on the tenth deck, as it was an to be an informal start.

Our cabin was on the fourth deck, which meant a long climb up the stairs. (We never ever use the lift, unless in an emergency, but never in an emergency.) Yes, we are the keep fit family.

As we made our way to the dining room, we pass the swimming pools and jacuzzis, and then we come to an abrupt stop. Before entering the dining room we have to go through the hand cleansing ritual, but there is nothing wrong with good hygiene.

As we enter, Sylvie's eyes open wide. Salads and veggie options galore. Meaty selection not too shabby either.

After we had our fill, we went to seek out the evening entertainment and of course, the cocktails. There is a certain pleasure knowing that the drinks are already paid for.

So with drinks in hand, we sat back in one of the lounges waiting to be entertained.

I don't know what we were expecting. A music band, yes. A music band from the Philippines, no. But they were very good and we enjoyed them all week.

They were followed by fun and games with the Thomson entertainment team, hilarious. Followed by more music.

Waiting for us, in our cabin is a copy of the Cruise News, the daily bulletin paper. This kept us up to date with what was going on, whether on shore, around the ship, and of course the evening entertainment.

So this evening there was a tribute to the group Queen in the Jubilee lounge, being big Freddy fans, this was a must.

We were not disappointed. The resident show team were amazing, a fantastic show. We went to see them every evening.

After Freddy and the team, it was time to go up on deck for a late night party. We gave it 20 minutes, but we were so tired we thought it was time to retire to our cabin.

By now, we had been cruising for around seven hours, and the ship hasn't moved an inch.

Just before midnight we heard a murmur and felt a slight vibration, we were leaving Tenerife. So with faces pressed against our cabin window, we watched our departure from the port. Next stop Gran Canaria.

Chapter 3
Gran Canaria

I don't know whether it was the excitement of the cruise, or the looking forward to going ashore, but I awoke early, too early, and we were still at sea. The sailing was so smooth, and the engines were very quiet, just a gentle hum.

I whispered to Sylvie, and we spent five minutes watching the wake leave the ship before falling back to sleep.

It's seven in the morning, and we were docked in the harbour at Las Palmas, Gran Canaria. With eager expectation and childlike excitement, we were looking forward to going ashore, but not before breakfast. Such a vast spread, but don't forget to wash your hands.

Time to go exploring on a guided tour. Whenever we left the ship, we had to get our boarding pass scanned and then on to a waiting coach.

I don't know what it is about being on a coach trip when middle-aged, middle-class cruise goers (do we call them mid-life cruisers?) are just one step away from turning into teenagers on a school trip. I blame the tour guide, our guide was so good, that the whole coach party were up for a good time.

Our first port of call was the local theatre. Why are modem theatres built like strange looking boxes? The best thing I can say about it was the location, right on the seafront.

One of the things we have found on all the Canary Islands we have visited is, being in the Atlantic, is that, even on a calm day, the waves come crashing in.

So when standing, camera in hand, with Sylvie posing, what background should use, a funny looking box or a wild seascape?

Move over Sylvie, I want the funny looking box with a wild seascape.

Time to move on. Back onto the coach. Next stop, the five-star Hotel Santa Catalina. We didn't qualify to enter the building, but we were given access to the grounds so that we could admire the architecture and the beautiful gardens. (Sylvie wants to go back).

Outside the hotel there is a statue of people standing on a rock, representing the Canarian people who would rather throw themselves into the sea than become slaves to the Spanish.

Off we go again. Time waits for no man, and nor does the guide. We are now going to the old town, where Christopher Columbus spent some time with 'Señora Columbus'.

After a short tour of the area passing the Canarian dogs, and avoiding the road race that was taking place, we were given a little free time, which we used going around the museum.

The only snag was that we never had enough time to have a proper look, as I had to rush Sylvie around much to her annoyance. Yes, we will come back.

Off we go again, I hope you are keeping up. We are now off to the highlight of our tour, the Caldera de Bandama, an extinct volcano that blew its top thousands of years ago, but the views are spectacular.

As we made our way, our guide was keeping in touch with other tour guides around the island, who are reporting rain, whilst we are enjoying the glorious sunshine. She was sounding so smug, but will it last?

The ride to the top was interesting if not scary, what with hairpin bends and sheer drops inches from the wheels, but they were still going around. It reminded me off the film *The Italian Job* (the original, of course).

Just as we reached the summit, it started to rain. I blamed the guide, who insisted on wearing boots and a raincoat. So what can you expect?

Quick! Take some photos, make it snappy, no time for posing, Sylvie. Get back on the coach, fly around the bends. To the ship and don't spare the horses.

We were just about to go aboard, when, stop! Don't forget to wash your hands, get our boarding passes scanned and put Sylvie's bag through the metal detector. With me getting into so much trouble, do you think I would let Sylvie anywhere near a weapon?

So we are back in time for lunch. The secret about mealtimes is not to eat too much. If you overindulge, mealtimes can lose their appeal and become a bit of a chore. So I decided to impress Sylvie and earn brownie points by having a salad with my beer.

After lunch, we had a bit of downtime, until suddenly, the sun came out. So we quickly abandoned ship and made our way to the promenade at Playa De Las Canteras. The sun was so warm we were having to take off coats and jackets as we watched the waves come crashing in. Yes, we will come back.

As we made our return to the ship, we just had to make a detour for our highlight of the day.

Anybody of a certain age will remember the clothing store, C&A. For us, it was a trip down memory lane. Just as we were leaving Sylvie spots a handbag shop. Apparently, there is no such thing as too many handbags. Another one to add to the collection.

We needed to be back on board by five thirty, so we had to get a move on. We were just approaching the ship when I got stopped.

A security guard decided he needed to see my boarding pass. Did I look as if I did not belong?

Back on board safe and sound. Time for the important things in life. Eating, drinking and entertainment. Sylvie said she could get used to this lifestyle.

Chapter 4
Day at Sea

A day of rest and relaxation. We woke up not knowing what day it was. We knew yesterday was Gran Canaria day and tomorrow is Madeira day. We haven't stopped since we left home on Thursday. Today must be Sunday.

Sylvie has kept us on a tight programme of events, with more to come, so it was quite nice to have a bit of a lay-in, and a leisurely breakfast, and not have to rush to catch a coach.

One of our main concerns was The Atlantic Ocean. We knew that when we were in the archipelago of the Canary Islands the waters would be relatively calm, but what about the mid-Atlantic?

We did not need to worry as the sea was flat calm. In fact, if we were further south you might have said that we were in the doldrums.

This morning it was time to explore the ship. Up till now there has been so much going on, we have had to run from one end of the ship to the other to keep up with the entertainment.

We found the Broadway shops, where the goods were reassuringly expensive, whereas the duty-free shop was dangerously priced. (I kept popping in, just to look. It was so tempting.) There was a library, a games' room, a casino, and my favourite place The Observation Lounge, which was a great place for pre-dinner drinks.

Meanwhile, this cruise also has a competitive edge, as Sylvie says I don't read enough. So after lunch, it's up on deck for some sunbathing and reading interspersed with live music from the resident band, and the Hi-de-Hi deck games and quizzes.

If you think this was all nice and relaxing, I wish it were. I had to sneak off to the celebration desk to make arrangements without Sylvie knowing, but then I am pretty good at slyness. And then it was late afternoon. The day was disappearing.

We had been invited to a cocktail reception with the Captain, followed by dinner. So out came the tux and bow tie and a cocktail dress for Sylvie. We don't usually do formal, we are ordinary people, but I'm a bit of a snob, so I think this is something we should do more often.

Anyway, all dressed up, we make our way to the Jubilee Lounge. It is quite disconcerting walking around a ship and passing people who are dressed casually when you are dressed up to the nines. Have we gone over the top?

We are reassured when we arrived and fitted in quite nicely, at least we looked as if we belonged.

We were asked if we would like a photo with the Captain. So we joined the queue. We knew he was Greek, and we love all things Greek, so this was a good omen.

"Kalimera, Captain," I say, shaking his hand. (Greek being my fourth language)

"Kalispera," the captain corrects me, as we pose for photos, with Sylvie putting us in the shade with her modelling skills.

Then, with a glass of champagne in hand, we make our way into the lounge, where the captain introduces himself and his officers, most of whom are Greek, which is reassuring.

The captain does a quick disappearing act, explaining that with so many Filipinos on his staff if they take over the bridge, we might find the ship on the way to the Philippines. We then made our way to our table for our five-course dinner.

At our table, we met a very nice couple of our age from South Wales who were on their third cruise, so we picked their brains for tips and ideas. Lovely couple.

Isn't it strange, how when you meet someone for the first time you then see them all the time, everywhere? This was true of our new cruise friends.

Meanwhile, we can't hang around, there are cocktails and entertainment to be found.

One thing we have learned whilst on this cruise, don't leave your cabin in the evening without your daily news sheet, which contains a vital entertainment programme.

So after taking part in a quiz, and having a singalong with the resident band, we all jump on stage and dance to an Abba tribute from the entertainment team.

Suddenly, it's midnight, and Sylvie has to do her Cinderella disappearing act, it's already too late for me as Sylvie says I resemble a pumpkin.

Goodnight, Sylvie.

Chapter 5
Funchal, Madeira

Well, here we go again. What has Sylvie got in store for us today?

Back to the early mornings and jumping on to a waiting coach. This island hopping is all very nice, but I do have one tiny complaint. As a sun lover, I haven't seen a lot. A little in Gran Canaria, but not much more.

For a long time now, Madeira has been on our bucket list of places to visit, and with a good friend of ours, Tracey, going there on a regular basis, we were looking forward to seeing it for ourselves. If only the sun would come out.

Hang on, what's this? Our first stop, half an hour looking at local fruit and veg and the leftover fish at the market. This was then followed by 20 minutes loitering around on a street corner. Great!

All aboard the coach again. Next stop, the Madeira Botanical Gardens. Paradise in the city.

This is a piece of land that was previously part of the estate belonging to the family of William Reid, the founder of the Reid's hotel. It was turned into a public garden and opened in 1960. Because of the mild climate, there are trees and plants from all over the world. Spectacular!

We can't hang around. There are more to see and do.

Suddenly, our coach has a near miss with a giant breadbasket, as it comes flying past us with four men grimly hanging on. We could not see the occupants of the said breadbasket as they were cowering under the blanket.

We were making our way to the cable car station, where we passed the start of the Wicker Toboggan Sled Ride, which looked downright dangerous. It did cross my mind to have a go so that I could write about it. Nah! I am one of those people who looks danger in the eye then runs away.

As I was saying, we were going on the cable car (a much safer option), which would take us back down to the port, which may sound straight forward, but a few years ago would have been a serious problem.

As I mentioned in chapter seven of 'Pura Vida', Sylvie has issues with heights. A few years ago, while in Barcelona, she dared herself to go in the cable car. She spent the whole journey glued to me. You could not get a cigarette paper between us. Now, in Funchal, she was sitting opposite me. Oh, how I miss Barcelona.

From point to point, this was a ten-minute journey over the houses and gardens, with our cruise ship getting ever closer.

Unfortunately, my eyes were drawn to the view directly below us. I don't think I have ever seen so many burnt out houses. I suddenly feel that I am not so keen on Funchal. (Tracey later told us of a major fire in 2016).

Our final port of call was not the port, but the Madeira port outlet. Heaven!

Before making our purchases we were able to partake of a couple of samples. Sylvie is not much of a drinker so cheers!

Strange as it may seem, although Sylvie is not a drinker, she does suffer from the side effects (knocking glasses off the table as she rises to leave the table). Never mind, girl.

Armed with our purchases, we made our way back to the ship. Hands washed. Bags x-rayed. Time for lunch.

By now, we were getting into the ship routine. Run around the port in the morning, chill and relax (chillax according to Adele) in the afternoon and party, party in the evening.

When I said chill I meant it literally as there was always a cool breeze blowing across the sun deck. This brings out a new game. The last man standing (or lazing on a sunbed).

So, not only am I in the reading stakes with Sylvie but now I am in the hide the goosebumps competition with everybody else.

Some make the excuse that it was three o'clock, time for afternoon tea, and so disappear. Sylvie said it was time for her nap, so off she went, but not me, I'll tough it out a bit longer.

Then I heard the siren call of the Royal Observation Lounge. It's a bit early for a cocktail so I settle for a beer, and at six o'clock I watched our departure from Madeira.

This evening's entertainment included a comedian, but before we check him out, we needed to go to the photo shop to check out the pictures from the evening before, you know, the ones with the captain.

Sylvie is not too sure, she is careful with money, (unless there is a handbag at stake). Not me, I scoop up all our prints, and hang the expense, they are memories. On to the show.

As I was saying, there is a comedian on tonight. We're not too sure about them, they can get a bit near the knuckle with their humour and language.

We did not need to worry, he was very good and his jokes were repeatable if only I could remember them.

Meanwhile, time goes sailing on.

Chapter 6
Happy Anniversary

Today is the day. Today is the reason for being here on this cruise. This was conceived on our odyssey to France. This was our landmark year (which is why we are all at sea) our 19th, you know, the one before the 20th, so this is the cruise before our cruise. I'm sure I've told you that we always do our homework. So this was to be our pre-cruise cruise. You see we are very thorough in our preparations.

I started the day by placing a well-chosen card on Sylvie's bedside. She values her sleep, so as we are still at sea, there is no hurry to wake her.

I then check today's newsletter, and yes, there is a little insert in the greetings section (who says I am not romantic?).

Just because it is our anniversary, it does not mean we can have a day off. Sylvie has plans for us, so when the ship docks we are ready for action.

Today we are on the island of La Palma, and we are going hiking at the Caldera de Taburiente National Park. We found out that the couple we met at the Captain's party was also on this visit. So we enjoyed their company and had a very pleasant afternoon in spectacular scenery, followed by a stop at a small café where I was able to practice my Spanish, (my third language, although Sylvie asks, "What is your first language?" cheeky!). It is quite reassuring when they understand what you are asking for.

So now, it was back to the ship for the main event. Before heading out for dinner, I had arranged a photo shoot, as we were dressed up, which was surprisingly fun, so spirits were high as we went to dinner.

All the time we were on board, we had our meals in the self-service restaurant, but not tonight. Tonight, I had booked a table at Le Bistro for à la carte dining experience.

When we arrived, we were shown to a suitably decorated table, with banners and balloons, and enjoyed a four-course meal accompanied by singing waiters, who were very amusing.

As Sylvie is not a drinker, she chose our liquid refreshment 'Mateus Rosé'. Very good, and to finish our meal in style, I had ordered a specially made anniversary cake, which we then had delivered to our cabin, while we went to enjoy the entertainment. Tonight, it was to be 'Cool Britannia'. The best of British music.

Not bad for the 19th. How am I going to top that next year? Watch this space.

Chapter 7
On Yer Bike!

After the high of yesterday comes the crash. Sometimes things and events can get over-planned. Some things can just turn around and bite you on the bum.

In the first place, Sylvie made an observation. Whilst I had taken particular care in choosing our cabin, it had a window, a double bed and was close to the stairs (for a quick getaway in an emergency), I had not taken into account what was going on outside our window.

Sylvie had noticed that every time we entered a port we were on the wrong side of the ship. Our view was not of the approaching island, but of the sea wall of the harbour, which all looked identical. It was as if the harbour wall was attached to the ship and we had brought it from island to island, and we could not see the actual island itself until we went on deck. What an oversight. Must get it right next time.

After this eye-opener, things went downhill (oh, if only) We were going to spend the morning cycling on El Hierro.

All kitted out with bike, helmet and water, we made our way on our ride along the coast.

Within five minutes, I was hit smack right in the face with a terrible flashback.

The last time Sylvie was on a bike was maybe five years ago, on a brand new bike that was too small for her which was evident when walkers were overtaking her. She was not best pleased.

Well, it did not take long for Sylvie to lag behind. The hills were not too bad if you used the gears if only Sylvie knew how to use them.

If guided by our cycle guide she was okay, if I tried to encourage her, head bitten off. Good job I've got plenty.

The route we took was along the coast which included a tunnel that was nearly a kilometre long and downhill. So when we all gathered together at the tunnel entrance, we waited for the lights to be in our favour, and then flew through the tunnel only to be told that have to come back the same way.

As we carried on, we could see in the distance a hotel, where we would have a break, if only Sylvie heard. We knew she hadn't heard because she and two others flew past the hotel. I had never seen her move so fast, but I would never dream of saying so, (I was down to my last head).

We had an hour stop at this hotel, for a rest and some refreshment, then it was back on the saddle.

Wasn't there a television commercial some years ago that had the tag line 'I'm not looking forward to the journey home either'? Not a truer word said.

Once you were past the tunnel, you were on the home straight, with a downhill stretch to the port.

But oh that tunnel! We were given two options. One, start walking on the sidewalk in the tunnel (hence the term push-bike). Option two was keep pedalling for as long as you could before getting off and walking.

"Is there not a third option?" someone asked, "Could we not take the road around the outside of the tunnel?"

"You could do, not recommended, there is a danger of falling boulders from the mountain. It might get messy."

Taking the hint, Sylvie starts walking, I'm on my bike and head off uphill. I got halfway when I am brought to a sudden halt by the cyclist in front who came to a wobbly end, and I lost all momentum and had to resort to the sidewalk.

After a ten-minute break at the exit of the tunnel, it was downhill back to the ship. I think if Sylvie had the strength she would pick up her bike and throw it into the harbour, and if I said anything I would have followed it. Did I say that it was Sylvie who organised our shore excursions? SPLASH!

After lunch, we followed our usual afternoon routine only this afternoon there was a sports memorabilia auction, so of course, I went along.

We were given ten minutes to check out the auction lots, there were poster prints, football shirts and boxing gloves (including a glove worn by Mohammed Ali).

I picked out a football shirt belonging to Frank Lampard of Chelsea, then checked out the room to see who my competition might be. I don't know why I bothered.

As the auction starts in earnest we were told that the minimum bid on these items was £100 (and that was for a print).

As the lots pass through there was not one taker. Then came the Frank Lampard shirt at a minimum bid of £175.

We have a bid, no, it was not me, I was too terrified to move a muscle, but someone did bid, sold! This was to be the highlight as no other lot was sold. (The reserved price for Mohammed Ali's boxing glove was £1,000.)

The day was going downhill fast, and there was more to come. After dinner, we went to look at our photos from the previous evening.

We were very pleased with the results. They were all of a very high standard. We wanted to take them all, but unfortunately, I got lost in the numbers.

There were 50 photos in total, which we could have on a disc for £6.99, (I paid £2.99 for a disc at home, so okay) and we could have one large print for £60.

I settle on buying the disc so that we could pick and choose in our own time, which one to enlarge. Everyone is happy until it came to paying.

"How much?" £6.99 turned into £699.

It seemed that I was the only one who did not understand the British money, so we left empty-handed and very disappointed. (They were beautiful pictures.)

I needed a drink and for this day to come to an end.

Chapter 8
What, No Lunch?

Today was to be the last full day of our cruise, and once we got on deck to see the island of La Gomera, we knew we were in for a treat.

We were based in the Valle Gran Rey, rising from the coast to the forested mountains, a most beautiful area.

If Tenerife had its glamour spots, then La Gomera had natural beauty, and this is what we had come to see for ourselves.

Having pushed the bikes to one side, we felt we were on firmer ground with hiking. We have a Border Collie, so spend hours walking.

Before our ten-kilometre hike, we needed to jump onto a coach with our guide. The scenery was spectacular as we made our way to the El Cedro Forest.

We were dropped off in the middle of nowhere, without a guide we would not have had a clue as to where we were or how to get back to our ship. So we played follow the leader through the beautiful forest.

Our guide spoke of a place in the forest where there was an abandoned church. We were hoping this would mean lunch and public conveniences.

When we got there, yes, there was a church, some picnic tables, even friendly birds looking for a free meal.

"We will stop here for one hour for lunch," said our guide.

"What lunch, we have no lunch."

"Excuse me, where are the toilets?" asked a somewhat desperate Sylvie.

"Over there," said the guide pointing to the trees.

We really are back to nature, but with no lunch, there was no point in staying here, so we made tracks and carried on with our hike, loving every minute.

Eventually, we met up with the coach, had it moved, or had we gone around in a circle, I will never know.

What I do know is that La Gomera has turned out to be one of our favourite islands, and yes, Sylvie, one day we will return.

In the meantime, it was our last evening of the cruise, time to say goodbye, but not before seeing the best show of the week, when the show team put on the West End Wonders show, culminating in a standing ovation.

Come the end of the cruise, our final verdict was that we did not fully know what was in store, we did not know if cruising was for us, but in the end, we loved it.

One month later, and we have already booked our next cruise for 2018 (our 20th anniversary) in Jamaica and the Caribbean.

Meanwhile, we still have three nights in Tenerife.

Chapter 9
Puerto De La Cruz

It's eight o'clock, we've arrived back in Santa Cruz, Tenerife, back to where it all started. While the majority of the guests are going home, Sylvie wanted more, so we booked three nights at the Hotel Catalonia Las Vegas in Puerto de la Cruz. So with a suitcase in hand, it's back to yet another coach.

As we dropped people off at various hotels on route, we gave the area and hotels a once over and decided they weren't for us. The hotels were nice (four and five-star), but they seemed to be in the middle of nowhere, miles from the beach and tourist hotspots.

When we arrived at our hotel, it was in the most perfect location, the area was buzzing. So we went to check-in which turned out to be a little embarrassing.

As we joined the queue at the reception, there seemed to be a delay and a lot of complaining. What was the fuss? As we neared the desk, we could see the problem.

Checking out time, twelve o'clock, noon. Checking in time, two o'clock. Time at present, eleven o'clock. Because of being on the cruise, everything was on tap, whatever you wanted, just turn up and it was available, now at the hotel, this was not the case. The guests had become spoilt and treated the hotel as part of the cruise, and so became embarrassingly rude to the staff.

When it came to our turn to check in, the situation was explained. We were able to leave our cases in a spare room, and explore the area. No problem.

When we got outside, we found ourselves in the most perfect location. Right on the seafront, with the promenade, cafés and bars right on the doorstep (it's always good to do your homework) as was the station for the road train that goes to Loro Parque.

We returned to our hotel, where we were able to complete our check-in, and went to our room, and wow! We had been given an upgrade to a superior room with a sea view (it always pays to be polite) and the Lago Martiánez pool complex right opposite. Fantastic.

So we sat on our balcony enjoying the sights and sounds whilst trying to read our novels (we were neck and neck on book two) until our stomachs told us it was time to eat. We were on half board so there was no need to go and peruse all the menus in town.

The dining room was enormous, as was the selection of dishes. The downside to this mass production from my point of view was that the chefs had lost heart so that it was like being in a staff canteen, there was no soul.

After eating, it was time to check out the nightlife. The shops were open the waiters were running around trying to keep up with their customers in the restaurants. There were singers and musicians in the bars, and British buskers on the promenade, the place had an atmosphere.

Sylvie then spotted a sign in a restaurant advertising 'Elvis' tomorrow night (I'll try to steer her away).

Actually, this was not our first visit to Puerto de la Cruz. Like most people, we had been to Tenerife a couple of times in the past, but staying down south of the island. On one occasion, we paid a visit and went to Loro Parque, which is what we were planning to do tomorrow.

On returning back to our hotel, it was straight back to our balcony, I knew the night view would be good and we were not disappointed. With the lights of the promenade, the pool complex and the other hotels, along with the sound of the crashing waves, I could have stayed on the balcony all night, but with plans for tomorrow, it was time to say goodnight.

Chapter 10
Loro Parque

We very nearly went to Loro Parque yesterday, but I just about managed to keep Sylvie under control.

Loro Parque is the sort of place you need to give plenty of time, as one of the top zoos in the world. It was a glorious day, warm and sunny, ideal.

After a speedy breakfast, it was straight out of the hotel onto the road train. I don't know what it is about land trains. When on holiday, we are all quick to jump on one, but back home we would be far too embarrassed to go near one.

There was no price for the road train, you just jump on. I guess the cost was swallowed up in the price of the entry cost.

Once inside, the memories came flooding back. The first thing that grabbed our attention was the bridge over the lake that was just teeming with koi carp. This had not changed in 25 years. Is it that long since we were last here?

There were highlights that we were looking forward to, the mainstays of the zoo, but they're also new ones. One of these was the penguin house.

As you enter the building, you step onto a travelator that takes you around an island surrounded by water, so you can watch the penguins swimming past you. There is also snow falling on the penguins on the island. This was a fantastic exhibit.

With so much to see and do, we had to keep a close eye on the time, with the parrot show, the dolphins and sea lions, and the killer whale show.

It was quite nostalgic seeing these shows after so many years. It was also very nice to see new species such as the white tiger.

The time just flew by, so as we went through the exit gate it was six o'clock, and the road train was waiting outside.

After such an energetic day, we decided to have a quiet evening, so after dinner, the hotel put on a circus act, which I thought was quite apt after our visit to the zoo.

The following day was our last full day. The sun was out again, it was the perfect day for sitting by the pool, topping up our tan (I could not go home without one), completing our books, generally being lazy.

Did we go for a dip in the pool? It was a quiet, peaceful day until someone went near the pool, you could hear them shrieking as they put a toe in the water, and that was the men, I'll just lie back and soak up the rays.

We thought we might eat out in the evening, so after our last stroll along the promenade, we found a beachfront restaurant for dinner.

In this particular restaurant, there was a large open space, that was soon filled with the locals who had come to dance. I mean real dancing, you know, the foxtrot, paso doble, even a tango, (we're strictly fans, don't you know).

After dinner, we made our way back to the hotel, just in time for the karaoke. I usually avoid these like the plague, but we are on holiday, so what the heck.

The room was packed, but there were only five people who took part, one of whom was ME.

My first was a Neil Diamond classic, followed by Adele (I had often bragged to Sylvie that I knew all the words to all the songs by Adele). Now was the time to prove it.

Later in the evening, an elderly lady with a hearing aid said she enjoyed my singing. Fame at last.

Chapter 11
Lost and Found

The time had come, we had been putting it off, but now it was time to go home.

We had a mid-morning transfer pickup, but the time we arrived at the airport time had moved on and we had to join the long queue for check-in.

I still had the issue of a lost mobile phone. After looking around the airport, and leaving Sylvie with the luggage, I could not find a Thomson desk. I was directed to a lost and found desk, but that was closed.

Sylvie's queue was getting short so my time was up, I had to get back. I thought that I might try further in London.

So after some last minute spends at the duty-free (focus out of view) we made our way onto the plane.

Whilst on our flight, we thought we might have a drink and a bite to eat. Not having much in the way of cash either in sterling or euros, we weren't worried, we would use card payment. Unfortunately, their card machine would not recognise our cards, so I had to hand over my muffin.

Once back at Gatwick Airport, it was a quick tour trying to find the Thomson desk. Once found, they were all closed. Never mind, let's try the lost and found. Success, there was someone there, someone to speak to.

"You will have to speak to the airport where you lost your mobile phone." I'll try tomorrow.

So it was back to the Airport Inn for the night. We love it there.

What's this? A room where the key works, and what's more, the restaurant was open, so after a nice meal and a drink, we settled downed ready for our train journey home.

The day after we got home, I spent all day on the phone trying to locate my mobile, with no success, so had to get a new one. So if you hear of a charity auction at the airport, you now know how they get the items for sale.

Oh! I think I need a holiday.

CPSIA information can be obtained
at www.ICGtesting.com
Printed in the USA
LVHW071657160320
650193LV00031B/834